M ARK TWAIN had lived most of
"translated" *The Diaries of Aa*
most lyrical and personal of all his
edition includes previously unpublish
mislaid final version of "Adam's Diary." And to fulfill Twain's
wish, the tales are gathered and told in alternating voices.

"*The sort of book that makes for deeply satisfying reading. For many readers familiar only with Twain's tales about mischievous boys or cranky vernacular characters, this work—one of the great love stories of all time—will come as a real surprise... This edition is proof that another look is more than warranted.*"
—The Mark Twain Forum

"*There is a sense of equality, feeling and wisdom that unfolds as a lesson on relationships...and becomes a truly noble treatment of gender and consequence.*
—Inside Pages

"*Funny? Yes. And you expect that from Mark Twain. But this is also a love story, something you wouldn't necessarily expect... At moments you realize that the story is being written by Samuel Clemens, the wounded human soul behind the sword and shield of Mark Twain.*"
—Birmingham Weekly

THE DIARIES OF ADAM & EVE

THE DIARIES OF
Translated by Mark Twain
ADAM & EVE

From Writings by MARK TWAIN

Edited by DON ROBERTS

Illustrated by MICHAEL MOJHER

FAIR OAKS PRESS / SAN FRANCISCO

FOR MAOMA YESSICK

Published by Fair Oaks Press, San Francisco

This edition combines "Extracts from Adam's Diary" and "Eve's Diary," with
passages from "Autobiography of Eve,"† "Eve Speaks," "That Day in Eden" and
"Adam's Soliloquy."

Library of Congress Cataloging-in-Publication Data
Twain, Mark, d 1835-1910.
    The diaries of Adam & Eve / c translated by Mark Twain ; edited and
    with an afterword by Don Roberts ; illustrated by Michael Mojher.
        p.   cm.
    ISBN 0-9658811-9-9 (acid-free paper)
    1.   2.
    I. Title.   II. Twain, Mark, 1835-1910.
III. Roberts, Don E.   IV. Mojher, Michael, ill.
PS1309   1997
813.4   97-60774

Library of Congress Catalog Card Number: 97-60774

First Paperback Edition, July 2001
Printed in the United States of America
10 9 8 7 6 5 4 3 2 1

Illustrations by Michael Mojher
Cover Design by Dotty Hardberger, Gabriel Design Group
Calligraphy by Kathy McNicholas
Back Cover Photograph by Thomas E. Marr: Mark Twain at Quarry Farm, 1902,
from the Collections of the Library of Congress.

Fair Oaks Press, Box 192871, San Francisco, CA 94119-2871
www.fairoakspress.com

Before he was Mark Twain, Sam Clemens had already been W. Epaminondas Adrastus Perkins, Josh, John Snooks and A Son of Adam. (The humorists of his day always wrote under a pen name; the more eccentric, the better.) If readers worried about their dogs going mad in August, A Son of Adam had the remedy: "Cut off their heads in July."

Throughout his long career, the idea of an Adam and an Eve intrigued Twain, but as an enduring fable rather than literal fact. While in the company of 150 pious Americans touring the Holy Land in 1867, he visited the traditional site of Adam's tomb in Jerusalem: "How touching it was, here in a land of strangers, far away from home and friends and all who cared for me, thus to discover the grave of a blood relation. True, a distant one, but still a relation."

Later on, as a lark, he would propose a monument to Adam. To his surprise, the idea won popular support, and Twain found himself petitioning Congress for assistance in its construction:

> *Mr. Darwin's Descent of Man had been in print five or six years, and the storm of indignation raised by it was still raging in pulpits and periodicals. In tracing the genesis of the human race back to its sources, Mr. Darwin had left Adam out altogether. We had monkeys, and "missing links," and plenty of other kinds of ancestors, but no Adam. . . . I said there seemed to be a likelihood that the world would discard Adam and accept the monkey, and that in the course of time Adam's very name would be forgotten in the earth; therefore this calamity ought to be averted; a monument would accomplish this. . . .*

Twain had intended to dedicate *Roughing It* (1871) "to the late Cain . . . it was his misfortune to live in a dark age that knew not

the beneficent Insanity Plea," but his brief inscription was reject-
ed by the publisher, who found it in poor taste.

Twain was clearly charmed by the idea that there had been a
first time for everything. He once noted "what a good thing Adam
had. When he said a good thing he knew nobody had said it
before." Leaving Adam and Eve virtually speechless, the author of
the biblical book of Genesis missed an opportunity that Twain
was only too happy to exploit, and in his Adam and Eve, curiosity and passion would have their beginnings.

In 1893, after completing the novel *Pudd'nhead Wilson,* he
wrote "Extracts from Adam's Diary," a short work he would revise
again and again. For a later edition, its preface read:

> [NOTE.—I translated a portion of this diary some years
> ago, and a friend of mine printed a few copies in an incom-
> plete form, but the public never got them. Since then I
> have deciphered some more of Adam's hieroglyphics, and
> think he has now become sufficiently important as a pub-
> lic character to justify this publication. —M.T.]

Twain went on to "translate" Eve's diary in 1905 and eventually
incorporated within it several new jottings by Adam. Although
both diaries were published separately as books, the author always
intended for the two to be united in one volume: "They score
points against each other—so, if not bound together, some of the
points would not be perceived. . . ."

This expanded edition merges the original, published diaries
and incorporates passages from his unfinished "Autobiography of
Eve†" as well as the lesser-known "Eve Speaks," "That Day in
Eden" and "Adam's Soliloquy." They are perhaps the most personal of Mark Twain's writings.

At First

EVE

WHO AM I? What am I? Where am I?[†]

SATURDAY

I am almost a whole day old now. I arrived yesterday. That is as it seems to me. And it must be so; for if there was a day before yesterday, I was not there when it happened, or I should remember it. It could be, of course, that it did happen and that I was not noticing. Very well, I will be watchful now, and if any day-before-yesterdays happen, I will make a note of it. It will be best to start right and not let the record get confused, for some instinct tells me that these details are going to be important to the historian someday.

11

I feel like an experiment; I feel exactly like an experiment. It would be impossible for a person to feel more like an experiment than I do, and so I am coming to feel convinced that that is what I *am*—an experiment, just an experiment and nothing more.

Then, if I am an experiment, am I the whole of it? No, I think not; I think the rest of it is part of it. I am the main part of it, but I think the rest of it has its share in the matter. Is my position assured, or do I have to watch it and take care of it? The latter, perhaps. Some instinct tells me that eternal vigilance is the price of supremacy. (That is a good phrase, I think, for one so young.)

Everything looks better today than it did yesterday. In the rush of finishing up, the mountains were left in a ragged condition, and some of the plains were so cluttered with rubbish and remnants that the aspects were quite distressing. Noble and beautiful works of art should not be subjected to haste, and this majestic new world is indeed a most noble and beautiful work. And certainly marvelously near to being perfect, notwithstanding the shortness of the time. There are too many stars in some places and not enough in others, but that can be remedied presently, no doubt.

I followed the other experiment around yesterday afternoon, at a distance, to see what it might be for, if I could. But I was not able to make it out. I think it is a man. I had never seen a man, but it looked like one, and I feel sure that that is what it is. I realize that I feel more curiosity about it than about any of the other reptiles. If it is a reptile, and I suppose it is, for it has frowsy hair and blue eyes and looks like a reptile. It has no hips; it tapers like a carrot. When it stands, it spreads itself apart like a derrick. So I think it is a reptile, though it may be architecture.

I was afraid of it at first and started to run every time it turned around, for I thought it was going to chase me. But by and by I found it was only trying to get away, so after that I was not timid anymore but tracked it along several hours, about twenty yards behind, which made it nervous and unhappy. At last it was a good deal worried and climbed a tree. I waited a good while, then gave it up and went home.

Today the same thing over. I've got it up the tree again.

MONDAY

*This new creature with the long hair is a good deal in the
way. It is always hanging around and following me about.
I don't like this; I am not used to company. I wish it would
stay with the other animals. . . .*

SUNDAY

It is up there yet. Resting, apparently. But that is a sub-
terfuge: Sunday isn't the day of rest; Saturday is appointed
for that. It looks to me like a creature that is more interested in resting than anything else. It would tire me to rest so
much. It tires me just to sit around and watch the tree. I do
wonder what it is for; I never see it do anything.

MONDAY

The moon got loose last night and slid down and fell out
of the scheme—a very great loss; it breaks my heart to think
of it. There isn't another thing among the ornaments and
decorations that is comparable to it for beauty and finish.
It should have been fastened better. If we can only get it
back again. . .

But, of course, there is no telling where it went. And
besides, whoever gets it will hide it; I know it, because I
would do it myself. I believe I can be honest in all other
matters, but I already begin to realize that the core and
center of my nature is love of the beautiful, a passion for the
beautiful, and that it would not be safe to trust me with
a moon that belonged to another person and that person

didn't know I had it. I could give up a moon that I found in the daytime, because I should be afraid someone was looking, but if I found it in the dark, I am sure I should find some kind of an excuse for not saying anything about it. For I do love moons, they are so pretty and so romantic. I wish we had five or six. I would never go to bed; I should never get tired lying out on the moss-bank and looking up at them.

Stars are good, too. I wish I could get some to put in my hair, but I suppose I never can. You would be surprised to find how far off they are, for they do not look it. When they first showed, I tried to knock some down with a pole, but it didn't reach, which astonished me. Then I tried clods till I was all tired out, but I never got one. It was because I am left-handed and cannot throw good. Even when I aimed at the one I wasn't after, I couldn't hit the other one, though I did make some close shots, for I saw the black blot of the clod sail right into the midst of the golden clusters forty or fifty times, just barely missing them. And if I could have held out a little longer, maybe I could have got one.

So I cried a little, which was natural, I suppose, for one of my age. And after I was rested, I got a basket and started for a place on the extreme rim of the circle, where the stars were close to the ground and I could get them with my hands, which would be better anyway because I could gather them tenderly then and not break them. But it was farther than I thought, and at last I had to give it up. I was so tired, I couldn't drag my feet another step; and besides, they were sore and hurt me very much.

I couldn't get back home; it was too far and turning cold. But I found some tigers and nestled in among them and was most adorably comfortable. And their breath was sweet and pleasant, because they live on strawberries. I had never seen a tiger before, but I knew them in a minute by the stripes.

TUESDAY

They returned the moon last night, and I was *so* happy! I think it is very honest of them. It slid down and fell off again, but I was not distressed. There is no need to worry when one has that kind of neighbors; they will fetch it back. I wish I could do something to show my appreciation. I would like to send them some stars, for we have more than we can use. I mean I, not we, for I can see that the reptile cares nothing for such things.

It has low tastes and is not kind. When I went there yesterday evening in the gloaming, it had crept down and was trying to catch the little speckled fishes that play in the pool, and I had to clod it to make it go up the tree again and let them alone. I wonder if *that* is what it is for? Hasn't it any heart? Hasn't it any compassion for those little creatures? Can it be that it was designed and manufactured for such ungentle work? It has the look of it. One of the clods took it back of the ear, and it used language. It gave me a thrill, for it was the first time I had ever heard speech, except my own. I did not understand the words, but they seemed expressive.

When I found it could talk, I felt a new interest in it, for I love to talk. I talk all day and in my sleep, too, and I am very interesting. But if I had another to talk to, I could be twice as interesting and would never stop, if desired.

If this reptile is a man, it isn't an *it*, is it? That wouldn't be grammatical, would it? I think it would be *he*. I think so. In that case one would parse it thus: nominative, *he;* dative, *him;* possessive, *his'n.* Well, I will consider it a man and call it he until it turns out to be something else. This will be handier than having so many uncertainties.

WEDNESDAY

I wish it would not talk; it is always talking. That sounds like a cheap fling at the poor creature, a slur, but I do not mean it so. I have never heard the human voice before, and any new and strange sound intruding itself here upon the solemn hush of these dreaming solitudes offends my ear and seems a false note. And this new sound is so close to me; it is right at my shoulder, right at my ear, first on one side and then on the other; and I am used only to sounds that are more or less distant from me.

THURSDAY

Today I am getting better ideas about distances. I was so eager to get hold of every pretty thing that I giddily grabbed for it, sometimes when it was too far off and sometimes when it was but six inches away, but seemed a foot—alas, with thorns between! I learned a lesson; also I made an axiom, all out of my own head—my first one: *The scratched experiment shuns the thorn.* I think it is a very good one for one so young.

TUESDAY

Cloudy today, wind in the east; think we shall have rain...
We? Where did I get that word?...I remember now—the
new creature uses it.

FRIDAY

My life is not as happy as it was.

SATURDAY

The new creature eats too much fruit. We are going to
run short most likely. "We" again—that is its *word; mine,*
too, now, from hearing it so much. Good deal of fog this
morning. I do not go out in the fog myself. The new crea-
ture does. It goes out in all weathers. And talks. It used to
be so pleasant and quiet here.

SUNDAY

All the week I tagged around after him and tried to get acquainted. I had to do the talking because he was so shy, but I didn't mind it. He seemed pleased to have me around, and I used the sociable "we" a good deal because it seemed to flatter him to be included.

SUNDAY

Pulled through. This day is getting to be more and more trying. It was selected and set apart as a day of rest. (I already had six of them per week before.)

WEDNESDAY

We are getting along very well indeed now and getting better and better acquainted. He does not try to avoid me anymore, which is a good sign, and shows that he likes to have me with him. That pleases me, and I study to be useful to him in every way I can, so as to increase his regard.

During the last day or two, I have taken all the work of naming things off his hands; and this has been a great relief to him, for he has no gift in that line and is evidently very grateful. He can't think of a rational name to save him, but I do not let him see that I am aware of his defect. Whenever a new creature comes along, I name it before he has time to expose himself by an awkward silence. In this way I have saved him many embarrassments.

I have no defect like his. The minute I set eyes on an animal, I know what it is. I don't have to reflect a moment; the right name comes out instantly, just as if it were an inspiration, as no doubt it is, for I am sure it wasn't in me half a minute before. I seem to know just by the shape of the creature and the way it acts what animal it is.

When the dodo came along, he thought it was a wild-cat—I saw it in his eye. But I saved him. And I was careful not to do it in a way that could hurt his pride. I just spoke up in a quite natural way of pleased surprise, and not as if I was dreaming of conveying information, and said: "Well, I do declare, if there isn't the dodo!" I explained—without seeming to be explaining—how I knew it for a dodo; and although I thought maybe he was a little piqued that I knew the creature when he didn't, it was quite evident that he admired me. That was very agreeable, and I thought of it more than once with gratification before I slept. How little a thing can make us happy when we feel that we have earned it.

ADAM

TUESDAY

I get no chance to name anything myself. The new creature names everything that comes along before I can get in a protest. And always the same pretext is offered—it looks *like the thing. There is the dodo, for instance. Says the moment one looks at it, one sees at a glance that it "looks like a dodo." It will have to keep that name, no doubt. It wearies me to fret about it, and it does no good anyway. Dodo! It looks no more like a dodo than I do.*

THURSDAY

My first sorrow. Yesterday he avoided me and seemed to wish I would not talk to him. I could not believe it and thought there was some mistake, for I loved to be with him and loved to hear him talk. And so how could it be that he could feel unkind towards me when I had not done anything? But at last it seemed true, so I went away and sat lonely in the place where I first saw him the morning that we were made and I did not know what he was and was indifferent about him. But now it was a mournful place, and every little thing spoke of him, and my heart was very sore. I did not know why very clearly, for it was a new feeling. I had not experienced it before, and it was all a mystery, and I could not make it out.

But when night came, I could not bear the lonesomeness and went to the new shelter he has built, to ask him what I had done that was wrong and how I could mend it and get back his kindness again. But he put me out in the rain, and it was my first sorrow.

THURSDAY

Built me a shelter against the rain, but could not have it to myself in peace. The new creature intruded. When I tried to put it out, it shed water out of the holes it looks with and wiped it away with the back of its paws, and made a noise such as some of the other animals make when they are in distress.

SUNDAY

It is pleasant again now and I am happy, but those were
heavy days. I do not think of them when I can help it.

MONDAY

The new creature says its name is Eve. That is all right, I have no objections. Says it is to call it by when I want it to come. I said it was superfluous then. The word evidently raised me in its respect; and indeed it is a large, good word and will bear repetition. It says it is not an It, it is a She. This is probably doubtful, yet it is all one to me. What she is were nothing to me if she would but go by herself and not talk.

Monday

This morning I told him my name, hoping it would interest him. But he did not care for it. It is strange. If he should tell me his name, I would care. I think it would be pleasanter in my ears than any other sound.

He talks very little. Perhaps it is because he is not bright and is sensitive about it and wishes to conceal it. It is such a pity that he should feel so, for brightness is nothing. It is in the heart that the values lie. I wish I could make him understand that a loving good heart is riches, and riches enough. And that without it, intellect is poverty.

Although he talks so little, he has quite a considerable vocabulary. This morning he used a surprisingly good word. He evidently recognized himself that it was a good one, for he worked it in twice afterward, casually. It was not good casual art, still it showed that he possesses a certain quality of perception. Without a doubt that seed can be made to grow, if cultivated.

Where did he get that word? I do not think I have ever used it.

No, he took no interest in my name. I tried to hide my disappointment, but I suppose I did not succeed. I went away and sat on the moss-bank with my feet in the water. It is where I go when I hunger for companionship, someone to look at, someone to talk to. It is not enough—that lovely white body painted there in the pool—but it is something, and something is better than utter loneliness. It talks when I talk; it is sad when I am sad; it comforts me with its sympathy. It says, "Do not be downhearted, you poor friendless girl, I will be your friend." It *is* a good friend to me, and my only one; it is my sister.

That first time that she forsook me! Ah, I shall never forget that—never, never. My heart was lead in my body! I said, "She was all I had, and now she is gone!" In my despair I said, "Break, my heart; I cannot bear my life anymore!" and hid my face in my hands, and there was no solace for me. And when I took them away after a little, there she was again, white and shining and beautiful. And I sprang into her arms!

That was perfect happiness. I had known happiness before, but it was not like this, which was ecstasy. I never doubted her afterward. Sometimes she stayed away—maybe an hour, maybe almost the whole day—but I waited and did not doubt. I said, "She is busy or she is gone a journey, but she will come." And it was so: She always did. At night she would not come if it was dark, for she was a timid little thing; but if there was a moon, she would come. I am not afraid of the dark. But she is younger than I am; she was born after I was. Many and many are the visits I have paid her. She is my comfort and my refuge when my life is hard—and it is mainly that.

SATURDAY

She fell into the pond yesterday when she was looking at herself in it, which she is always doing. She nearly strangled and said it was most uncomfortable.

This made her sorry for the creatures which live in there, which she calls fish, for she continues to fasten names onto things that don't need them and don't come when they are called by them, which is a matter of no consequence to her, as she is such an unreflecting and irrelevant half-blown bud anyway; so she got a lot of them out and brought them in last night and put them in my bed to keep warm, but I have noticed them now and then all day, and I don't see that they are any happier there than they were before, only quieter.

When night comes I shall throw them outdoors. I will not sleep with them again, for I find them clammy and unpleasant to be among when a person hasn't anything on.

TUESDAY

All the morning I was at work improving the estate, and I purposely kept away from him in the hope that he would get lonely and come. But he did not.

At noon I stopped for the day and took my recreation by flitting all about with the bees and the butterflies and reveling in the flowers, those beautiful creatures that catch the smile of God out of the sky and preserve it! I gathered them and made them into wreaths and garlands and clothed myself in them while I ate my luncheon—apples, of course. Then I sat in the shade and wished and waited. But he did not come.

No matter. Nothing would have come of it, for he does not care for flowers. He calls them rubbish and cannot tell one from another and thinks it is superior to feel like that. He does not care for me, he does not care for flowers, he does not care for the painted sky at eventide—is there anything he does care for except building shacks to coop himself up in from the good clean rain and thumping the melons and sampling the grapes and fingering the fruit on the trees to see how those properties are coming along?

I laid a dry stick on the ground and tried to bore a hole in it with another one in order to carry out a scheme that I had, and soon I got an awful fright. A thin, transparent bluish film rose out of the hole, and I dropped everything and ran! I thought it was a spirit, and I *was* so frightened! But I looked back and it was not coming, so I leaned against a rock and rested and panted and let my limbs go on trembling until they got steady again. Then I crept warily back, alert, watching and ready to fly if there was occasion. And when I was come near, I parted the branches of a rosebush and peeped through—wishing the man was about, I was looking so cunning and pretty—but the sprite was gone. I went there, and there was a pinch of delicate pink dust in the hole. I put my finger in, to feel it, and said *ouch!* and took it out again. It was a cruel pain. I put my finger in my mouth; and by standing first on one foot and then the other and grunting, I presently eased my misery. Then I was full of interest and began to examine it.

I was curious to know what the pink dust was. Suddenly the name of it occurred to me, though I had never heard of it before. It was *fire!* I was as certain of it as a person could be of anything in the world. So without hesitation, I named it that—fire.

I had created something that didn't exist before; I had added a new thing to the world's uncountable properties. I realized this and was proud of my achievement and was going to run and find him and tell him about it, thinking to raise myself in his esteem—but I reflected and did not do it.

No—he would not care for it. He would ask what it was good for, and what could I answer? For it was not *good* for something, but only beautiful, merely beautiful. . .

So I sighed and did not go, for it wasn't good for anything. It could not build a shack; it could not improve melons; it could not hurry a fruit crop. It was useless. It was a foolishness and a vanity. He would despise it and say cutting words. But to me it was not despicable. I said, "Oh, you fire, I love you, you dainty pink creature, for you are *beautiful*—and that is enough!" and was going to gather it to my breast. But refrained. Then I made another maxim out of my own head, though it was so nearly like the first one that I was afraid it was only a plagiarism: *The burnt experiment shuns the fire.*

I wrought again; and when I had made a good deal of fire-dust, I emptied it into a handful of dry brown grass, intending to carry it home and keep it always and play with it. But the wind struck it, and it sprayed up and spat out at me fiercely, and I dropped it and ran. When I looked back the blue spirit was towering up and stretching and rolling away like a cloud; and instantly I thought of the name of it—*smoke!*—though, upon my word, I had never heard of smoke before.

Soon, brilliant yellow-and-red flares shot up through the smoke, and I named them in an instant—*flames!*—and I was right, too, though these were the very first flames that had ever been in the world. They climbed the trees, they flashed splendidly in and out of the vast and increasing volume of tumbling smoke, and I had to clap my hands and laugh and dance in my rapture, it was so new and strange and so wonderful and so beautiful!

He came running and stopped and gazed and said not a word for many minutes. Then he asked what it was. Ah, it was too bad that he should ask such a direct question. I had to answer it, of course, and I did. I said it was fire. If it annoyed him that I should know and he must ask, that was not my fault. I had no desire to annoy him. After a pause he asked, "How did it come?"

Another direct question, and it also had to have a direct answer. "I made it."

The fire was traveling farther and farther off. He went to the edge of the burned place and stood looking down and said, "What are these?"

"Fire-coals."

He picked up one to examine it, but changed his mind and put it down again. Then he went away. *Nothing* interests him.

But I was interested. There were ashes, gray and soft and delicate and pretty—I knew what they were at once. And the embers; I knew the embers, too. I found my apples and raked them out and was glad, for I am very young and my appetite is active. But I was disappointed; they were all burst open and spoiled. Spoiled apparently—but it was not so: They were better than raw ones. Fire is beautiful; someday it will be useful, I think.

FRIDAY

I saw him again for a moment last Monday at nightfall, but only for a moment. I was hoping he would praise me for trying to improve the estate, for I had meant well and had worked hard. But he was not pleased and turned away and left me.

He was also displeased on another account: I tried once more to persuade him to stop going over the falls. That was because the fire had revealed to me a new passion—quite new and distinctly different from love, grief and those others which I had already discovered—*fear*. And it is horrible! I wish I had never discovered it. It gives me dark moments, it spoils my happiness, it makes me shiver and tremble and shudder. But I could not persuade him, for he has not discovered fear yet, and so he could not understand me.

FRIDAY

She has taken to beseeching me to stop going over the falls. What harm does it do? Says it makes her shudder. I wonder why. I have always done it—always liked the plunge and the excitement and the coolness. I supposed it was what the falls were for. They have no other use that I can see, and they must have been made for something. She says they were only made for scenery—like the rhinoceros and the mastodon.

I am too much hampered here. What I need is a change of scene.

FRIDAY

Tuesday—Wednesday—Thursday—and today: all without seeing him. It is a long time to be alone; still it is better to be alone than unwelcome.

I *had* to have company—I was made for it, I think—so I made friends with the animals. They are just charming, and they have the kindest dispositions and the politest ways. They never look sour, they never let you feel that you are intruding. They smile at you and wag their tail, if they've got one, and they are always ready for a romp or an excursion or anything you want to propose. I think they are perfect gentlemen. All these days we have had such good times, and it hasn't been lonesome for me, ever. Lonesome! No, I should say not. Why, there's always a swarm of them around—sometimes as much as four or five acres—you can't count them. And when you stand on a rock in the midst and look out over the furry expanse, it is so mottled and splashed and gay with color and frisking sheen and sun-flash, and so rippled with stripes, that you might think it was a lake, only you know it isn't. And there's storms of sociable birds and hurricanes of whirring wings; and when the sun strikes all that feathery commotion, you have a blazing up of all the colors you can think of, enough to put your eyes out.

We have made long excursions, and I have seen a great deal of the world. Almost all of it, I think. And so I am the first traveler—and the only one. When we are on the march, it is an imposing sight; there's nothing like it anywhere. For comfort, I ride a tiger or a leopard because it is soft and has a round back that fits me and because they are such pretty animals. But for long distance or for scenery, I ride the elephant. He hoists me up with his trunk, but I can get off myself: When we are ready to camp, he sits and I slide down the back way.

The birds and animals are all friendly to each other, and there are no disputes about anything. They all talk, and they all talk to me. But it must be a foreign language, for I cannot make out a word they say; yet they often understand me when I talk back, particularly the dog and the elephant. It makes me ashamed. It shows that they are brighter than I am and are therefore my superiors. It annoys me, for I want to be the principal experiment myself—and I intend to be, too.

SATURDAY

I escaped last Tuesday night and traveled two days and built me another shelter in a secluded place and obliterated my tracks as well as I could. But she hunted me out by means of a beast, which she has tamed and calls a wolf, and came making that pitiful noise again and shedding that water which she calls tears. I was obliged to return with her, but will presently emigrate again, when the occasion offers.

She engages herself in many foolish things: among others, trying to study out why the animals called lions and tigers live on grass and flowers when, as she says, the sort of teeth they wear would indicate that they were intended to eat each other.

THURSDAY

I have learned a number of things and am educated now, but I wasn't at first. I was ignorant at first. At first, it used to vex me, because with all my watching, I was never smart enough to be around when the water was running uphill. But now I do not mind it. I have experimented and experimented until now I know it never does run uphill, except in the dark. I know it does in the dark, because the pool never goes dry, which it would, of course, if the water didn't come back in the night.

It is best to prove things by actual experiment. Then you *know;* whereas if you depend on guessing and supposing and conjecturing, you will never get educated.

Some things you *can't* find out, but you will never know you can't by guessing and supposing. No, you have to be patient and go on experimenting until you find out that you can't find out. And it is delightful to have it that way; it makes the world so interesting. If there wasn't anything to find out, it would be dull. Even trying to find out and not finding out is just as interesting as trying to find out and finding out, and I don't know but more so. The secret of the water was a treasure until I *got* it; then the excitement all went away, and I recognized a sense of loss.

By watching, I know that the stars are not going to last. I have seen some of the best ones melt and run down the sky. Since one can melt, they can all melt; since they can all melt, they can all melt the same night. That sorrow will come—I know it. I mean to sit up every night and look at them as long as I can keep awake. And I will impress those sparkling fields on my memory so that by and by when they are taken away, I can by my fancy restore those lovely myriads to the black sky and make them sparkle again. And double them by the blur of my tears.

SUNDAY

Pulled through.

MONDAY

I believe I see what the week is for: It is to give time to rest up from the weariness of Sunday. It seems a good idea.

TUESDAY

She told me she was made out of a rib taken from my body. This is at least doubtful, if not more than that. I have not missed any rib. . . .

She is in much trouble about the buzzard; says grass does not agree with it, is afraid she can't raise it, thinks it was intended to live on decayed flesh. The buzzard must get along the best it can with what it is provided. We cannot overturn the whole scheme to accommodate the buzzard.

SUNDAY

Pulled through.

Thursday

*Perhaps I ought to remember that she is very young, a mere
girl, and make allowances. She is all interest, eagerness,
vivacity. The world is to her a charm, a wonder, a mystery,
a joy. She can't speak for delight when she finds a new
flower; she must pet it and caress it and smell it and talk to
it and pour out endearing names upon it.*

*And she is color-mad: brown rocks, yellow sand, gray
moss, green foliage, blue sky—the pearl of the dawn, the
purple shadows on the mountains, the golden islands float-
ing in crimson seas at sunset, the pallid moon sailing through
the shredded cloud-rack, the star-jewels glittering in the
wastes of space.*

*None of them is of any practical value so far as I can
see. But because they have color and majesty, that is enough
for her, and she loses her mind over them.*

*If she could quiet down and keep still a couple of
minutes at a time, it would be a reposeful spectacle. In
that case, I think I could enjoy looking at her. Indeed I am
sure I could, for I am coming to realize that she is a quite
remarkably comely creature—lithe, slender, trim, rounded,
shapely, nimble, graceful. And once, when she was standing
marble-white and sun-drenched on a boulder, with her
young head tilted back and her hand shading her eyes,*

watching the flight of a bird in the sky, I recognized that she was beautiful.

MONDAY

It is a joy to be so beautiful. And Adam—he is the same. When I have flowers on my head, it is better still.

THURSDAY

Today, in a wood, we heard a voice.

We hunted for it, but could not find it. Adam said he had heard it before, but had never seen it, though he had been quite close to it. So he was sure it was like the air and could not be seen. I asked him to tell me all he knew about the voice, but he knew very little. It was Lord of the Garden, he said, and had told him to dress the garden and keep it; and it had said we must not eat of the fruit of a certain tree and that if we ate of it we should surely die. Our death would be certain. That was all he knew.

I wanted to see the tree, so we had a pleasant long walk to where it stood alone in a secluded and lovely spot; and there we sat down and looked long at it with interest and talked. Adam said it was the tree of knowledge of good and evil.

"Good and evil?"

"Yes."

"What is that?"

"What is what?"

"Why, those things. What is good?"

"I do not know. How should I know?"

"Well, then, what is evil?"

"I suppose it is the name of something, but I do not know what."

"But Adam, you must have *some* idea of what it is."

"*Why* should I have some idea? I have never seen the thing; how am I to form any conception of it? What is your own notion of it?"

Of course I had none, and it was unreasonable of me to require him to have one. There was no way for either of us to guess what it might be. It was a new word, like the other; we had not heard them before, and they meant nothing to us. My mind kept running on the subject, and presently I said, "Adam, there are those other words—die and death. What do *they* mean?"

"I have no idea."

"Well, then, what do you *think* they mean?"

"My child, cannot you see that it is impossible for me to make even a plausible *guess* concerning a matter about which I am absolutely ignorant? A person can't *think* when he has no material to think *with*. Isn't that true?"

"Yes, I know it, but how vexatious it is. Just because I can't know, I all the more *want* to know."

We sat silent awhile turning the puzzle over in our minds. Then all at once I saw how to find out and was surprised that we had not thought of it in the beginning, it was so simple. I sprang up and said, "How stupid we are! Let us eat of it. We shall die, and then we shall know what it is and not have any more bother about it."

Adam saw that it was the right idea, and he rose at once and was reaching for an apple when a most curious creature came floundering by, of a kind which we had never seen before, and of course we dropped a matter that was of no special scientific interest to rush after one that *was*.

Miles and miles over hill and dale we chased that lumbering, scrambling, fluttering goblin till we were away down the western side of the valley where the pillared great banyan tree is; and there we caught him. What a joy, what a triumph: He is a pterodactyl! [†]

ADAM

MONDAY

If there is anything on the planet that she is not interested in, it is not in my list. There are animals that I am indifferent to, but it is not so with her. She has no discrimination. She takes to all of them. She thinks they are all treasures; every new one is welcome.

When the mighty brontosaurus came striding into camp, she regarded it as an acquisition. I considered it a calamity. That is a good sample of the lack of harmony that prevails in our views of things. She wanted to domesticate it; I wanted to make it a present of the homestead and move out. She believed it could be tamed by kind treatment and would be a good pet; I said a pet twenty-one feet high and eighty-four feet long would be no proper thing to have about the place, because even with the best intentions and without meaning any harm, it could sit down on the house and mash it, for anyone could see by the look of its eye that it was absentminded.

Still, her heart was set upon having that monster, and she couldn't give it up. She thought we could start a dairy with it and wanted me to help her milk it. But I wouldn't; it was too risky. The sex wasn't right, and we hadn't any ladder anyway. Then she wanted to ride it and look at the scenery. Thirty or forty feet of its tail was lying on the ground like a fallen tree, and she thought she could climb it, but she was mistaken: When she got to the steep place, it was too slick and down she came, and would have hurt herself but for me.

Was she satisfied now? No. Nothing ever satisfies her but demonstration; untested theories are not in her line, and she won't have them. She was born scientific. It is the right spirit, I concede it. It attracts me; I feel the influence of it. If I were with her more, I think I should take it up myself.

Well, she had one theory remaining about this colossus: She thought that if we could tame him and make him friendly, we could stand him in the river and use him for a bridge. It turned out that he was already plenty tame enough—at least as far as she was concerned—so she tried her theory, but it failed: Every time she got him properly placed in the river and went ashore to cross over on him, he came out and followed her around like a pet mountain. Like the other animals. They all do that.

TUESDAY

She has taken up with a snake now. Nothing comes amiss to her in the animal line. She trusts them all, they all trust her; and because she wouldn't betray them, she thinks they won't betray her. I am glad because the snake talks, and this enables me to get a rest.

FRIDAY

She says the snake advises her to try the fruit of that tree and says the result will be a great and fine and noble education.

THURSDAY

I tried to get him some of those apples. I failed, but I think the good intention pleased him. They are forbidden, and he says I shall come to harm. But so I come to harm through pleasing him, why shall I care for that harm?

TUESDAY

She has been climbing that tree again. She said nobody was looking. Seems to consider that a sufficient justification for chancing any dangerous thing. Told her that. The word justification moved her admiration—and envy, too, I thought. It is a good word.

I advised her to keep away from the tree. She said she wouldn't. I foresee trouble. Will emigrate.

WEDNESDAY

Escaped that night and rode a horse as fast as he could go, hoping to get clear out of the garden and hide in some other country before the disaster should fall. But it was not to be. About an hour after sunup, as I was riding through a flowery plain where thousands of animals were grazing, slumbering or playing with each other according to their wont, all of a sudden they broke into a tempest of frightful noises, and in one moment the plain was a frantic commotion and every beast was destroying its neighbor.

I knew what it meant: Eve had eaten that fruit, and death was come into the world.... The tigers ate my horse, paying no attention when I ordered them to desist, and they would even have eaten me if I had stayed—which I didn't.

I found this place outside the garden, but she has found me out. In fact, I was not sorry she came, for there are but meager pickings here, and she brought some of those apples. I was obliged to eat them, I was so hungry. It was against my principles, but I find that principles have no real force except when one is well fed. . . .

She came curtained in boughs and bunches of leaves, and when I asked her what she meant by such nonsense and snatched them away and threw them down, she tittered and blushed. I had never seen a person titter and blush before, and to me it seemed unbecoming and foolish. She said I would soon know how it was myself.

This was correct. Hungry as I was, I laid down the apple half-eaten and arrayed myself in the discarded boughs and branches, and then spoke to her with some severity and ordered her to go and get some more and not make such a spectacle of herself. She did it, and after this we crept down to where the wild-beast battle had been and collected some skins, and I made her patch together a couple of suits proper for public occasions. They are uncomfortable, it is true, but they are in the mode, and that is the main point about clothes. . . .

I find she is a good deal of a companion. I see I should be lonesome and depressed without her, now that I have lost my property. Another thing, she says it is ordered that we work for our living hereafter. She will be useful. I will superintend.

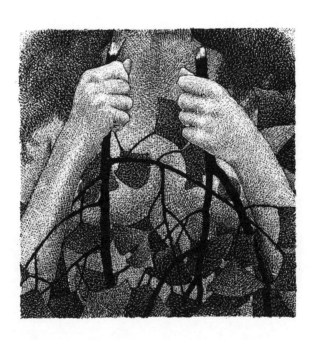

AFTER THE FALL

WHEN I LOOK BACK, the garden is a dream to me. It was beautiful, surpassingly beautiful, enchantingly beautiful. And now it is lost, and I shall not see it anymore.

The garden is lost, but I have found *him* and am content. He loves me as well as he can. I love him with all the strength of my passionate nature, and this, I think, is proper to my youth and sex.

If I ask myself why I love him, I find I do not know and do not really much care to know; so I suppose that this kind of love is not a product of reasoning and statistics, like one's love for other reptiles and animals. I think that this must be so.

I love certain birds because of their song, but I do not love Adam on account of his singing—no, it is not that.

The more he sings, the more I do not get reconciled to it. Yet I ask him to sing because I wish to learn to like everything he is interested in. I am sure I can learn, because at first I could not stand it, but now I can. It sours the milk, but it doesn't matter; I can get used to that kind of milk.

It is not on account of his brightness that I love him—no, it is not that. He is not to blame for his brightness, such as it is, for he did not make it himself. He is as God made him, and that is sufficient. There was a wise purpose in it; *that* I know. In time it will develop, though I think it will not be sudden; and besides, there is no hurry. He is well enough just as he is.

It is not on account of his gracious and considerate ways and his delicacy that I love him. No, he has lacks in these regards, but he is well enough just so and is improving.

It is not on account of his industry that I love him—no, it is not that. I think he has it in him, and I do not know why he conceals it from me. It is my only pain. Otherwise he is frank and open with me, now. I am sure he keeps nothing from me but this. It grieves me that he should have a secret from me, and sometimes it spoils my sleep, thinking of it. But I will put it out of my mind; it shall not trouble my happiness, which is otherwise full to overflowing.

It is not on account of his education that I love him—no, it is not that. He is self-educated and does really know a multitude of things. But they are not so.

It is not on account of his chivalry that I love him—no, it is not that. He told on me. But I do not blame him; it is a peculiarity of sex, I think, and he did not make his sex. Of course, I would not have told on him; I would have perished first, but that is a peculiarity of sex, too, and I do not take credit for it, for I did not make my sex.

Then why is it that I love him? *Merely because he is masculine,* I think.

At bottom, he is good; and I love him for that, but I could love him without it. If he should beat me and abuse me, I should go on loving him. I know it. It is a matter of sex, I think.

He is strong and handsome, and I love him for that, and I admire him and am proud of him, but I could love him without those qualities. If he were plain, I should love him; if he were a wreck, I should love him. And I would work for him and slave over him and pray for him and watch by his bedside until I died.

Yes, I think I love him merely because he is *mine* and is *masculine.* There is no other reason, I suppose. And so I think it is as I first said: that this kind of love is not a product of reasonings and statistics. It just *comes*—none knows whence—and cannot explain itself. And doesn't need to.

It is what I think. But I am only a girl and the first that has examined this matter; and it may turn out that in my ignorance and inexperience I have not got it right.

A Year Later

We have named it Cain. She caught it while I was up country trapping, caught it in the timber a couple of miles from our dugout—or it might have been four, she isn't certain which. It resembles us in some ways and may be a relation. That is what she thinks, but this is an error, in my judgment.

The difference in size warrants the conclusion that it is a different and new kind of animal—a fish perhaps, though when I put it in the water to see, it sank, and she plunged in and snatched it out before there was an opportunity for the experiment to determine the matter. I still think it is a fish, but she is indifferent about what it is and will not let me have it to try. I do not understand this.

The coming of the creature seems to have changed her whole nature and made her unreasonable about experiments. She thinks more of it than she does of any of the other animals, but is not able to explain why. Her mind is disordered—everything shows it.

Sometimes she carries the fish in her arms half the night when it complains and wants to get to the water. At such times the shining water drops trickle down her face, and she pats the fish on the back and makes soft sounds with her mouth to soothe it and betrays sorrow and solicitude in a hundred ways. I have never seen her do like this with any other fish, and it troubles me greatly. She used to carry the young tigers around so and play with them, before we lost our property; but it was only play. She never took on about them like this when their dinner disagreed with them.

THURSDAY

When he had been gone a week, little Cain was born. It was a great surprise to me; I was not aware that anything was going to happen. But it was just as Adam is always saying: "It is the unexpected that happens."

I did not know what to make of it at first. I took it for an animal. But it hardly seemed to be that, upon examination, for it had no teeth and hardly any fur and was a singularly helpless mite. Some of its details were human, but there were not enough of them to justify me in scientifically classifying it under that head. Thus it started as a *lusus naturae*—a freak—and it was necessary to let it go at that, for the time being, and wait for developments.

However, I soon began to take an interest in it, and this interest grew day by day. Presently, this interest took a warmer cast and became affection, then love, then idolatry; and all my soul went out to this creature, and I was consumed with a passion of gratitude and happiness. Life was become a bliss, a rapture, an ecstasy; and I longed day by day, hour by hour, minute by minute for Adam to return and share my almost unendurable joy.

At last he came, but he did not think it was a child. He meant well and was dear and lovely, but he was scientist first and man afterward—it was his nature—and he could accept nothing until it was scientifically proven.

The alarms I passed through with that student's experiments are quite beyond description. He exposed the child to every discomfort and inconvenience he could imagine in order to determine what kind of bird or reptile or quadruped it was and what it was for, and so I had to follow him about, day and night, in weariness and despair to appease its poor little sorrows and help it to bear them the best it could. †

SUNDAY

She doesn't work Sundays, but lies around all tired out and likes to have the fish play over her. And she makes foolish noises to amuse it and pretends to chew its paws, and that makes it laugh. I have not seen a fish before that could laugh. That makes me doubt.... I have come to like Sunday myself. Superintending all the week tires a body so. There ought to be more Sundays.

THURSDAY

Adam wakes up. Asks me not to forget to set down those four new words. It shows he has forgotten them. But I have not. For his sake I am always watching. They are down. It is he that is building the dictionary—so *he* thinks—but I have noticed that it is I who do the work. It is no matter; I like to do anything that he wants me to do. And in the case of the dictionary, I take special pleasure in the labor because it saves him a humiliation, poor boy. His spelling is unscientific. He spells cat with a *k* and catastrophe with a *c,* although both are from the same root. [†]

WEDNESDAY

It isn't a fish.

I cannot quite make out what it is. It makes curious, vicious noises when not satisfied and says "goo-goo" when it is. It is not one of us, for it doesn't walk; it is not a bird, for it doesn't fly; it is not a frog, for it doesn't hop; it is not a snake, for it doesn't crawl. I feel sure it is not a fish, though I cannot get a chance to find out whether it can swim or not. It merely lies around, and mostly on its back with its feet up. I have not seen any other animal do that before. I said I believed it was an enigma, but she only admired the word without understanding it. I never had a thing perplex me so.

THREE MONTHS LATER

The perplexity augments instead of diminishing. I sleep but little. It has ceased from lying around and goes about on its four legs now. Yet it differs from the other four-legged animals in that its front legs are unusually short, consequently this causes the main part of its person to stick up uncomfortably high in the air, and this is not attractive.

It is built much as we are, but its method of traveling shows that it is not of our breed. The short front legs and long hind ones indicate that it is of the kangaroo family, but it is a marked variation of the species, since the true kangaroo hops, whereas this one never does. Still, it is a curious and interesting variety and has not been catalogued before. As I discovered it, I have felt justified in securing the credit of the discovery by attaching my name to it and hence have called it Kangaroorum Adamiensis. . . .

It must have been a young one when it came, for it has grown exceedingly since. It must be five times as big now as it was then; and when discontented, it is able to make from twenty-two to thirty-eight times the noise it made at first. Coercion does not modify this, but has the contrary effect. For this reason I discontinued the system. She reconciles it by persuasion and by giving it things which she had previously told it she wouldn't give it.

As already observed, I was not at home when it first came, and she told me she found it in the woods. It seems odd that it should be the only one; yet it must be so, for I have worn myself out these many weeks trying to find another one to add to my collection and for this one to play with. For surely then it would be quieter and we could tame it more easily. But I find none, nor any vestige of any; and strangest of all, no tracks. It has to live on the ground; it cannot help itself. Therefore, how does it get about without leaving a track? I have set a dozen traps, but they do no good. I catch all small animals except that one—animals that merely go into the trap out of curiosity, I think, to see what the milk is there for. They never drink it.

THURSDAY

I scored the next great triumph for science myself: to wit,
how the milk gets into the cow. Both of us had marveled
over that mystery a long time. We had followed the cows
around—that is, in the daytime—but had never caught
them drinking a fluid of that color. And so at last we said
they undoubtedly procured it at night. Then we took turns
and watched them by night. The result was the same—the
puzzle remained unsolved. These proceedings were of a sort
to be expected in beginners, but one perceives now that they
were unscientific. A time came when experience had taught
us better methods.

One night as I lay musing and looking at the stars, a
grand idea flashed through my head, and I saw my way! My
first impulse was to wake Adam and tell him, but I resisted
it and kept my secret. I slept not a wink the rest of the night.
The moment the first pale streak of dawn appeared, I flitted
stealthily away; and deep in the woods I chose a small grassy
spot and wattled it in, making a secure pen. Then I enclosed
a cow in it. I milked her dry, then left her there a prisoner.
There was nothing there to drink—she must get her milk by
her secret alchemy or stay dry.

All day I was in a fidget—and could not talk connect-
edly, I was so preoccupied—but Adam was busy trying to

invent a multiplication table and did not notice. Toward sunset he had got as far as 6 times 9 are 27, and while he was drunk with the joy of his achievement and dead to my presence and all things else, I stole away to my cow. My hand shook so with excitement and with dread of failure that for some moments I could not get a grip on a teat. Then I succeeded, and the milk came! Two gallons. Two gallons, and nothing to make it out of. I knew at once the explanation: *The milk was not taken in by the mouth, it was condensed from the atmosphere* through the cow's hair. I ran and told Adam, and his happiness was as great as mine, and his pride in me inexpressible.

Presently he said, "Do you know, you have not made merely one weighty and far-reaching contribution to science, but two."

And that was true. By a series of experiments we had long ago arrived at the conclusion that atmospheric air consisted of water in invisible suspension; also that the components of water were hydrogen and oxygen, in the proportion of two parts of the former to one of the latter and expressible by the symbol H_2O. My discovery revealed the fact that there was still another ingredient: milk. We enlarged the symbol to H_2OM. [†]

One Month Later

The kangaroo still continues to grow, which is very strange and perplexing. I never knew one to be so long in getting its growth. It has fur on its head now—not like kangaroo fur, but exactly like our hair, except that it is much finer and softer and, instead of being black, is red.

I am like to lose my mind over the capricious and harassing developments of this unclassifiable zoological freak. If I could catch another one—but that is hopeless. It is a new variety and the only sample; this is plain.

But I caught a true kangaroo and brought it in, thinking that this one, being lonesome, would rather have that for company than have no kin at all, or any animal it could feel a nearness to or get sympathy from in its forlorn condition here among strangers who do not know its ways or habits, or what to do to make it feel that it is among friends. But it was a mistake—it went into such fits at the sight of the kangaroo that I was convinced it had never seen one before.

I pity the poor noisy little animal, but there is nothing I can do to make it happy. If I could tame it—but that is out of the question. The more I try, the worse I seem to make it. It grieves me to the heart to see it in its little storms of sorrow and passion. I wanted to let it go, but she wouldn't

*hear of it. That seemed cruel and not like her, and yet
she may be right. It might be lonelier than ever, for since I
cannot find another one, how could* it?

Five Months Later

*It is not a kangaroo. No, for it supports itself by holding
to her finger and thus goes a few steps on its hind legs and
then falls down. It is probably some kind of a bear, and
yet it has no tail—as yet—and no fur, except on its head.
It still keeps on growing—that is a curious circumstance,
for bears get their growth earlier than this. Bears are
dangerous—since our catastrophe—and I shall not be satisfied to have this one prowling about the place much longer
without a muzzle on.*

*I have offered to get her a kangaroo if she would let this
one go, but it did no good; she is determined to run us into
all sorts of foolish risks, I think. She was not like this before
she lost her mind.*

A Fortnight Later

*I examined its mouth. There is no danger yet; it has only
one tooth. It has no tail yet. It makes more noise now than*

it ever did before—and mainly at night. I have moved out. But I shall go over mornings, to breakfast and to see if it has more teeth. If it gets a mouthful of teeth, it will be time for it to go, tail or no tail, for a bear does not need a tail in order to be dangerous.

THURSDAY

He believed I had found it in the woods, and I was glad and grateful to let him think so, because the idea beguiled him to go away at times and hunt for another, and this gave the child and me blessed seasons of respite and peace. No one can ever know the relief I felt whenever he ceased from his distressful experiments and gathered his traps and bait together and started for the woods.

As soon as he was out of sight, I hugged my precious to my heart and smothered it with kisses and cried for thankfulness. The poor little thing seemed to realize that something fortunate for us had happened, and it would kick and crow and spread its gummy mouth and smile the happy smile of childhood all the way down to its brains—or whatever those things are that are down in there. †

ADAM

ONE MONTH LATER

I have been off hunting and fishing a month. Meantime, the bear has learned to paddle around all by itself on its hind legs and says "poppa" and "momma." It is certainly a new species. This resemblance to words may be purely accidental, of course, and may have no purpose or meaning; but even in that case, it is still extraordinary and is a thing which no other bear can do. This imitation of speech, taken together with general absence of fur and entire absence of tail, sufficiently indicates that this is a new kind of bear.

The further study of it will be exceedingly interesting. Meantime, I will go off on a far expedition and make an exhaustive search. There must certainly be another one somewhere, and this one will be less dangerous when it has company of its own species. I will go straightaway, but I will muzzle this one first.

THURSDAY

At first I couldn't make out what I was made for. But now I think it was to search out the secrets of this wonderful world and be happy and thank the giver of it all for devising it. I think there are many things to learn yet—I hope so; and by economizing and not hurrying too fast, I think they will last weeks and weeks. I hope so.

By experiment, I know that wood swims—and dry leaves and feathers and plenty of other things. Therefore, by all that cumulative evidence, you know that a rock will swim; but you have to put up with simply knowing it, for there isn't any way to prove it—up to now. But I shall find a way—then *that* excitement will go. Such things make me sad, because by and by when I have found out everything, there won't be any more excitements, and I do love excitements so! The other night I couldn't sleep for thinking about it.

When you cast up a feather, it sails away on the air and goes out of sight; then you throw up a clod, and it doesn't. It comes down every time. I have tried it and tried it, and it is always so. I wonder why it is? Of course it *doesn't* come down, but why should it *seem* to? I suppose it is an optical illusion. I mean, one of them is. I don't know which one. It may be the feather, it may be the clod.

I can't prove which it is; I can only demonstrate that one or the other is a fake and let a person take his choice.

Three Months Later

It has been a weary, weary hunt, yet I have had no success. In the meantime, without stirring from the home estate, she has caught another one! I never saw such luck. I might have hunted these woods a hundred years, I never should have run across that thing.

Next Day

I have been comparing the new one with the old one, and it is perfectly plain that they are the same breed. I was going to stuff one of them for my collection, but she is prejudiced against it for some reason or other. So I have relinquished the idea, though I think it is a mistake. It would be an irreparable loss to science if they should get away.

The old one is tamer than it was and can laugh and talk like the parrot, having learned this, no doubt, from being with the parrot so much and having the imitative faculty in a highly developed degree. I shall be astonished if it turns out to be a new kind of parrot; and yet I ought not to be astonished, for it has already been everything else it could think of since those first days when it was a fish.

The new one is as ugly now as the old one was at first, has the same sulphur-and-raw-meat complexion and the same singular head without any fur on it. She calls it Abel.

YEAR SIX

Cain and Abel are beginning to learn. Already Cain can add as well as I can, and multiply and subtract a little. Abel is not as quick as his brother mentally; but he has persistence, and that seems to answer in the place of quickness. Abel learns about as much in three hours as Cain does, but Cain gets a couple of hours out of it for play. So Abel is a long time on the road; but as Adam says, he "arrives on schedule just the same." Adam has concluded that persistence is one of the talents and has classified it under that head in his dictionary. [†]

YEAR TEN

They are boys; we found it out long ago. It was their coming in that small, immature shape that puzzled us; we were not used to it. There are some girls now. Abel is a good boy, but if Cain had stayed a bear it would have improved him.

YEAR TWELVE

We have nine children now. Cain and Abel are dear little chaps, and they take very nice care of their little brothers and sisters. The four eldest of the flock go wandering everywhere, according to their desire, and often we see nothing of them for two or three days together.

Once they lost Gladys and came back without her. They could not remember just where or when it was that they missed her. It was far away, they said, but they did not know how far; it was a new region for them. It was rich in berries of the plant which we call the deadly nightshade—for what reason we do not know. It hasn't any meaning, but it utilizes one of the words which we long ago got of the voice, and we like to employ new words whenever a chance offers and so make them workable and handy. They are fond of those berries, and they long wandered about, eating them. By and by when they were ready to go somewhere else, they missed Gladys, and she did not answer to her name.

Next day, she did not come. Nor the next day, nor the day after that. Then three more days, and still she did not come. It was very strange; nothing quite the match of this had ever happened before. Our curiosity began to be excited. Adam was of the opinion that if she did not come next day, or at furthest the day after, we ought to send Cain and Abel to look.

So we did that. They were gone three days, but they found her. She had had adventures. In the dark the first night, she fell in the river and was washed down a long distance, she did not know how far, and was finally flung upon a sandbar. After that, she lived with a kangaroo's family and was hospitably entertained, and there was much sociability. The mama-kangaroo was very sweet and motherly, and would take her babies out of her pocket and go foraging among the hills and dales and fetch home a pocketful of the choicest fruits and nuts. And nearly every night there was company—bears and rabbits and buzzards and chickens and foxes and hyenas and polecats and other creatures—and gay romping and grand times. The animals seemed to pity the child because she had no fur; for always when she slept they covered her with leaves and moss to protect her dainty flesh, and she was covered like that when the boys found her. She had been homesick the first days, but had gotten over it.

That was her word—homesick. We have put it in the dictionary and will presently settle upon a meaning for it. It is made of two words which we already had and which have clear meanings when by themselves, though apparently none when combined. Building a dictionary is exceedingly interesting work—but tough, as Adam says.

Several days ago, little Abel found a clover with four leaves. Naturally it caused great excitement. Adam could hardly believe his eyes, yet there it was: that impossible thing. There it was—and moreover, possible. Adam said there might be others; it wasn't likely, but there might be. So the first thing in the morning, we started, the eager children scampering on ahead, Cain and Abel in the lead, little Gladys and Edwina toddling after. . . .[†]

YEAR TWELVE

After all these years, I see that I was mistaken about Eve in the beginning; it is better to live outside the garden with her than inside it without her. At first I thought she talked too much, but now I should be sorry to have that voice fall silent and pass out of my life.

Blessed be the sorrow that brought us near together and taught me to know the goodness of her heart and the sweetness of her spirit!

YEAR TWENTY

It is a day and a night now that he has slept. We found him lying by his altar in his field that morning, his face and body drenched in blood. He said his eldest brother struck him down. Then he spoke no more and fell asleep. We laid him in his bed and washed the blood away and were glad to know the hurt was light and that he had no pain, for if he had had pain he would not have slept.

Adam comes.

"Well?"

"He still sleeps," answers Adam.

"He has slept enough for his good, and his garden suffers for his care. Wake him."

"I have tried and cannot."

"Then he is very tired. Let him sleep on."

"I think it is his hurt that makes him sleep so long."

I answer: "It may be so. Then we will let him rest; no doubt the sleep is healing it."

It was in the early morning that we found him. All day he slept that sweet, reposeful sleep, lying always on his back and never moving, never turning. It showed how tired he was, poor thing. That is our second-born—our Abel. He is so good and works so hard, rising with the dawn and laboring till the dark. And now he is overworked; it will be best that he tax himself less after this. And I will ask him; he will do anything I wish.

That Night

All the day he slept. I know, for I was always near and made dishes for him and kept them warm against his waking. Often I crept in and fed my eyes upon his gentle face and was thankful for that blessed sleep. And still he slept on—slept with his eyes wide, a strange thing, and made me think he was awake at first. But it was not so, for I spoke and he did not answer. He always answers when I speak. Cain has moods and will not answer, but not Abel.

I have sat by him all the night, being afraid he might wake and want his food. His face was very white, and it changed, and he came to look as he had looked when he was a little child . . . so sweet and good and dear. It carried me back over the abyss of years, and I was lost in dreams and tears—oh, hours, I think. Then I came to myself and, thinking he stirred, I kissed his cheek to wake him, but he slumbered on and I was disappointed. His cheek was cold.

I brought sacks of wool and the down of birds and covered him, but he was still cold, and I brought more. Adam has come again and says he is not yet warm. I do not understand it.

Next Day

We cannot wake him! With my arms clinging about him, I have looked into his eyes, through the veil of my tears, and begged for one little word, and he will not answer. Oh, is it that long sleep—is it death? And will he wake no more?

One Week Later

They drove us from the garden with their swords of flame, the fierce cherubim. And what had we done? We meant no harm. We were ignorant and did as any other children might do. We could not know it was wrong to disobey the command, for the words were strange to us and we did not understand them. We did not know right from wrong— how should we know? We could not, without the Moral Sense; it was not possible. If we had been given the Moral Sense first—ah, that would have been fairer, that would have been kinder. Then we should be to blame if we disobeyed. But to say to us poor ignorant children words which we could not understand and then punish us because we did not do as we were told—ah, how can that be justified? We knew no more then than this littlest child of mine knows now with its four years—oh, not so much,

I think. Would I say to it, "If thou touchest this bread, I will overwhelm thee with unimaginable disaster, even to the dissolution of thy corporeal elements," and when it took the bread and smiled up in my face, thinking no harm, not understanding those strange words, would I take advantage of its innocence and strike it down with the mother-hand it trusted? Whoso knoweth the mother-heart, let him judge if I would do that thing.

Adam says my brain is turned by my troubles and that I am become wicked. I am as I am; I did not make myself.

FORTY YEARS LATER

It is my prayer, it is my longing, that we may pass from this life together—a longing which shall never perish from the earth, but shall have place in the heart of every wife that loves, until the end of time. And it shall be called by my name.

But if one of us must go first, it is my prayer that it shall be I. For he is strong, I am weak. I am not so necessary to him as he is to me. Life without him would not be life; how could I endure it? This prayer is also immortal and will not cease from being offered up while my race continues. I am the first wife, and in the last wife I shall be repeated.

AT EVE'S GRAVE

Wheresoever she was; there *was Eden.*

IN THE PRESENT DAY

AFTER INSPECTING THE DINOSAUR EXHIBIT in the American Museum of Natural History, New York City, Adam is resting on a bench in Central Park, "mid-afternoon, dreamily noting the drift of the species back and forth."

To think this multitude is but a wee little fraction of the earth's population! And all blood-kin to me, every one! Eve ought to have come with me. This would excite her affectionate heart. She was never able to keep her composure when she came upon a relative; she would try to kiss every one of these people, black and white and all.

A young mother approaches, pushing a baby carriage. She draws it to the bench, sits down near Adam and begins to push the carriage "softly back and forth with one hand...."

How little change one can notice—none at all, in fact. I remember the first child well—let me see . . . it is three-hundred thousand years ago come Tuesday. This one is just like it. So between the first one and the last one there is really nothing to choose. The same insufficiency of hair, the same absence of teeth, the same feebleness of body and apparent vacancy of mind, the same general unattractiveness all around.

Yet Eve worshiped that early one, and it was pretty to see her with it. This latest one's mother worships it; it shows in her eyes—it is the very look that used to shine in Eve's. To think that so subtle and intangible a thing as a look could flit and flash from face to face down a procession three-hundred thousand years long and remain the same, without shade of change! Yet here it is, lighting this young creature's face just as it lighted Eve's in the long ago—the newest thing I have seen in the earth, and the oldest.

"**I** SAW HER FIRST... in her brother Charley's stateroom in the steamer *Quaker City,* in the Bay of Smyrna, in the summer of 1867, when she was in her twenty-second year." So Sam Clemens would describe the glimpse of a cameo photograph of Olivia Langdon, while he was anchored off the coast of Turkey. He said he had loved her from then on; but as for marriage, he had also said, "I wouldn't have a girl *I* was worthy of. *She* wouldn't be respectable enough."

Worthiness aside, Olivia was better than respectable enough: A delicate beauty, she was the devout, classics-educated daughter of Elmira, New York's first family. Ten years her senior, Clemens was a redheaded rascal who came out of small-town poverty in Hannibal, Missouri. His formal education had ended at age thirteen (later than he would have preferred), and a brush with Sunday school had left him with only "a trained Presbyterian conscience." Then thirty-two, the newspaper correspondent was becoming famous as Mark Twain, author of "Jim Smiley and His Jumping Frog," a yarn syndicated to American newspapers; and he had started his first book, *The Innocents Abroad,* an account of the *Quaker City's* voyage to Europe and the Holy Land.

They met in New York City several months later; and on New Year's Eve, Clemens accompanied the Langdons to a reading by Charles Dickens, then concluding his second American tour. Dickens's career was at its end, Clemens's just beginning.

The evening also marked the beginning of a long courtship. Although Olivia turned down his proposal of marriage three times, he continued to woo her by letter—184 letters that she called "the loveliest love letters that ever were written." He begged her to reform him and make him worthy: "Give me a little room in that great heart of yours...and if I fail to deserve it, may I remain forever the homeless vagabond I am!" Persuasive, he was; and she eventually said yes. He always called her Livy:

> Livy, you are as kind and good and sweet and unselfish and just, and truthful, and sensible and intellectual as the homeliest woman I ever saw (for you know that these qualities belong peculiarly to homely women). I have so longed for these qualities in my wife, and have so grieved because she would have to be necessarily a marvel of ugliness—I who do worship beauty. But with a good fortune which is a very miracle, I have secured these things in my little wife to be—and beauty— beauty beyond any beauty that I ever saw in a face before.

They married two years later, four children followed, and they built their home at Nook Farm, a community of friendly intellectuals in Hartford and a place conducive to his writing. *The Adventures of Tom Sawyer, The Prince and the Pauper* and *Adventures of Huckleberry Finn* followed. Livy would always be the first to read what he wrote: "Ever since we have been married, I have been dependent on my wife to go and revise my manuscript....I can do the spelling and grammar alone but I don't always know just where to draw the line in matters of taste. Mrs. Clemens has kept a lot of things from getting into print that might have given me a reputation I wouldn't care to have."

He lost fortunes as quickly as he made them, and in 1891 the family moved to Europe, where what remained of their wealth went further. By then Mark Twain was as celebrated abroad as Dickens had been in America, and they lived as expatriates for most of the next nine years. To make ends meet, he regularly dispatched manuscripts to his American publishers.

In 1892 at the Villa Viviani near Florence, he completed *Pudd'nhead Wilson* and then started "Extracts from Adam's Diary."

He declared the story "a little gem if I *do* say it myself" and mailed it off to *Cosmopolitan* magazine. They turned it down.

For *The Niagara Book,* a collection of essays promoting the falls to tourists, he revised "Adam's Diary," adding references to Buffalo, Lake Erie and Tonawanda to create "the earliest authentic mention of Niagara Falls." His original version would see print just once, in the 1897 British edition of *Tom Sawyer, Detective.*

Twain modeled Adam after himself, endowing the first man with, among other attributes, the laziness that he often (and almost proudly) owned up to: "I am no lazier now than I was forty years ago, but that is because I reached the limit forty years ago. You can't go beyond possibility." In fact, he was a prolific writer who happened to regard his work as play.

In 1901, he began an "autobiography" of Eve. It was a natural follow-up to his *Personal Recollections of Joan of Arc* completed five years earlier—and would become as difficult a project. Describing the trials of completing *Joan of Arc,* he said, "There are some books that refuse to be written. They stand their ground year after year and will not be persuaded. It isn't because the book is not there and worth being written—it is only because the right form for the story does not present itself." After numerous false starts, Eve's story refused to tell itself, and he put it aside. The unfinished manuscripts combine Eve's commentary with diary entries that follow civilization through the first millenium, beyond the flood to the earth's overpopulation.

By 1903, Livy's always-fragile health began to decline, and because the doctors believed her husband's presence caused "psychological distress," he was ordered to keep his distance. She would neither see him nor hear his voice for the better part of the next two years, except in the occasional, five-minute visit. They communicated by notes delivered between his writing room and her sickroom. To her, he was never Sam, he was Youth:

Youth my own precious Darling, I feel so frightfully banished. Couldn't you write in my boudoir? Then I could hear you clear your throat and it would be such joy to feel you near. I miss you sadly, sadly. Your note in the morning gave me support for the day, the one at night, peace for the night. With the deepest love of my heart, your Livy.

Don't know the date nor the day. But anyway, it is a soft and pensive foggy morning, Livy darling, and the naked tree branches are tear-beaded, and Nature has the look of trying to keep from breaking down and sobbing, poor old thing. Good morning, dear heart, I love you dearly. 'Y.'

Youth darling, have you forgotten your promise to me? You said that you would not publish what I would disapprove....Think of the side I know—the sweet, dear, tender side—that I love so. Why not show this more to the world. Does it help the world to always rail at it?...Oh I love you so and wish you would listen and take heed.

Livy darling, precious little comforter. You have cast out the devil that possessed me for the present and all is well. I have kept the promises and obeyed the instructions. All is well—all will be well.

With bankruptcy, the unexpected death of their eldest child, and Livy's illness and isolation, his writings had grown darker, more bitter, more cynical. Clemens had always felt reluctant to serve his reader anything but the shenanigans expected of the great Mark Twain—the humorist—and had even contemplated publishing

The Prince and the Pauper anonymously, fearing that it would be too refined for his readers. It was her favorite.

Livy's health improved, and a milder climate was recommended to speed her recovery. As plans were made, he wrote to her: "It is good to think of a quiet retreat in a suburb of Florence. Yes, I am glad we are going to Italy. You will get well there." But six months later, on June 5, 1904, Livy died at the Villa di Quarto in the Italian countryside. She was fifty-eight years old. In a letter to her brother, Clemens wrote: "I am a man without a country. Wherever Livy was, that was my country."

Afterward, he returned to his homeland and, in the seclusion of New Hampshire, found the right form for Eve's story: "Eve's love story, but we will not call it that." This was "Eve's Diary," as he called it, a sentimental companion piece to Adam's comic chronicle—and it was Livy's eulogy. Then and only then did he write from the woman's point of view. The story was published in the Christmas 1905 issue of *Harper's*.

For a hardbound, illustrated edition of "Extracts from Adam's Diary" in 1904, Twain had deleted every reference to Niagara Falls and made other revisions: Where Adam had once called Eve a "numskull," she became "an unreflecting and irrelevant half-blown bud." Where Eve had blamed their banishment from Eden on Adam's sense of humor, Twain ignored the issue of blame entirely. But the adulterated "Niagara Falls" version was printed by mistake, and Twain's revisions would be forgotten.

Eve's Diary was similarly published as a book in 1906, but to its closing pages he added several new passages from Adam's diary. Their tales conclude at Eve's grave, where Adam's solitary presence reflects the writer's own loneliness. He allows Adam the last word, a tender expression of the gravity of love and loss.

Eve's Diary included fifty-four illustrations by Lester Ralph, with Eve depicted in "summer costume." (One of them is included here.) The stir they created in Worcester, Massachusetts, led to the book's being banned there, to which Twain responded: "It appears that the pictures in *Eve's Diary* were first discovered by a lady librarian. It took her some time to examine them all, but she did her hateful duty! I don't blame her for this careful examination; the time she spent was, I am sure, enjoyable, for I found considerable fascination in them myself."

Twain had reviewed the fate of Adam and Eve again and again, but mostly in quick sketches written and put aside. In "Eve Speaks," Eve—more woman than girl—rages over the loss of Eden and the death of Abel. In "Adam's Soliloquy," Adam revisits the earth aeons later to spend an afternoon in New York City, only to discover how little his offspring have evolved. Finally, in 1909, Twain began *Letters from the Earth*, a scorching treatise on morality and religion. With Satan as its narrator, the story of Adam and Eve follows a course that revealed the author's own despair: "So the First Pair went forth from the Garden under a curse—a permanent one." Not intended for publication, *Letters from the Earth* was never completed.

He continued to hope the two diaries would be published together, just as he longed to be with Livy. Sam Clemens had been born under the glow of Halley's Comet in the night sky, and he once said, "It will be the greatest disappointment of my life if I don't go out with Halley's Comet." He died at sundown, April 21, 1910, one day before the comet reached perihelion, its closest proximity to the sun. He was seventy-four years old.

In *My Mark Twain,* published a few months later, William Dean Howells remembered Clemens and Livy:

> I make bold to speak of the love between them, because without it I could not make him known to others as he was known to me. It was a greater part of him than the love of most men for their wives, and she merited all the worship he could give her, all the devotion, all the implicit obedience, by her surpassing force and beauty of character. She

was in a way the loveliest person I have ever seen, the gentlest, the kindest, without a touch of weakness; she united wonderful tact with wonderful truth; and Clemens not only accepted her rule implicitly, but he rejoiced, he gloried in it . . . if there was any forlorn and helpless creature in the room Mrs. Clemens was somehow promptly at his side or hers . . . she loved to let her heart go beyond the reach of her hand, and imagined the whole hard and suffering world with compassion for its structural as well as incidental wrongs. . . . But this kindness went with a sense of humor which qualified her to appreciate the self-lawed genius of a man who will be remembered with the great humorists of all time, with Cervantes, with Swift, or with any others worthy his company; none of them was his equal in humanity. . . . He was a youth to the end of his days, the heart of a boy with the head of a sage; the heart of a good boy, or a bad boy, but always a wilful boy, and wilfulest to show himself out at every time for just the boy he was.

Sam Clemens gave life and immortality to Tom Sawyer, Becky Thatcher, Huck Finn, the slave Jim, Tom Canty, Hank Morgan and, perhaps his finest creation, Mark Twain. Of his and Livy's four children, only one would outlive them. And today there are no descendents of this son of Adam and his Eve.

—Don E. Roberts

This book is an edited compilation of passages from Mark Twain's Adamic diaries. In order to create a harmonious narrative from six works written over a period of a dozen years, the editor has deleted several words and sentences, and repositioned entries from the longer works. The original paragraphing and punctuation were modified and spellings updated for consistency's sake. Otherwise, these are Twain's words, just as he wrote them.

The sources identified below, with page references to this book, will help the interested reader identify each diary entry. (Adam is generally represented by Twain's final, preferred version of his diary extracts.)

"Extracts from Adam's Diary," 1893 (published in *The Niagara Book),* 1897 (in the British edition of *Tom Sawyer, Detective, as Told by Huck Finn and Other Tales)* and 1904 (as *Extracts from Adam's Diary*): 14, 21, 23, 25, 28, 30, 32, 36, 44, 47, 50, 59–60, 62–64, 73–74, 77, 79–81, 84–86, 88, 93–94, 96 and 100.

"Autobiography of Eve[†]" (and its continuation), written around 1901, first published in *The Bible According to Mark Twain,* Baetzhold and McCullough, University of Georgia Press, Athens, 1995: 11 (line 1), 55–57, 75–76, 78, 82–83, 87, 95 and 97–99.

"Eve Speaks" (originally "Passage from Eve's Diary"), written in 1901, published in *Europe and Elsewhere,* 1923: 101–106.

"That Day in Eden" (originally "Passage from Satan's Diary"), written in 1901, published in *Europe and Elsewhere,* 1923: 55 (lines 1–2).

"Adam's Soliloquy," written in 1905, published in *Europe and Elsewhere,* 1923: 113–114.

"Eve's Diary," 1905 (in *Harper's*), 1906 (as *Eve's Diary*): 11–13, 17–20, 22, 24, 26–27, 29, 31, 33–35, 39–43, 45–46, 48–49, 51–52, 58–59, 61, 69–72, 89–90, 106 and 109.

From the beginning, Mark Twain has been our pilot.

The hardcover edition of the *Diaries* was published in late 1997 in what was expected to be a single printing. We remain grateful for the help and encouragement of these good people: Michael Mojher, who illustrated the story so perfectly; Brenda Coker and Bob Hirst, the Mark Twain Project at the University of California, Berkeley; Dotty Hardberger of the Gabriel Design Group, the jacket designer; Jennifer Brathovde in the Prints and Photographs Division, the Library of Congress; Bob Greenebaum and Karl Frauhammer of McNaughton & Gunn, our printer; Ward Anderson; Marina Bacchetti; Brian Buchanan; Heidi Butenschoen; Kerrie Chappelka; Tina Freschi and Darin Steinberg; Gail Friedlander; Veronica Gaynor; Pati and Sara Hoskins; Larry Howe; Betsy Howkinson; Karen Joffe; Elspeth Martin; Carla Morris; Judith Schenck; Pam Utz; and Chuck Williams.

Once in print, a book must be nurtured if it's to reach the first reader. This happens in bookstores, most often in independent bookstores, and we remain grateful to those booksellers who were the first to take the *Diaries* to heart and give it precious space on their shelves: Faith Bell of Bell's Books; Jeff Dolman, Cover to Cover Booksellers; Stacy Furrer, Fifth Avenue Books; Jake Reiss, Alabama Booksmith; Brian Rood, Avenue Books; Kevin Ryan, Green Apple Books; Bonnie Stuppin, Alexander Book Company; and Carrie Thiederman, A Clean Well-Lighted Place for Books.

Finally, there are Elaine Anderson, Ann Spivack, Karen Bornstein and Gary Jones. As Twain put it, "To get the full measure of a joy, you must have someone to share it with."

The Diaries of Adam & Eve: Translated by Mark Twain is also available as an audiobook on cassette and compact disc. Performed by Mandy Patinkin and Betty Buckley, with Walter Cronkite narrating, this is audio literature at its best.

Best Spoken Word Album
Grammy Award Nomination

Best Multi-Voiced Narration
Audie Award Winner

Annual Listen-Up Award
Publishers Weekly

"An enchanting re-creation of Mark Twain's Diaries of Adam and Eve!"
—"All Things Considered," National Public Radio

"This one is a treasure. In it, we hear the voice of Mark Twain as he imagines the beginning of humankind and explores the differences between men and women. And we hear the voice of Walter Cronkite as he describes Twain's life and work in the afterword. The performances of Betty Buckley and Mandy Patinkin do justice to Twain's work. You'll want to listen to this one more than once."
—The Roanoke Times

"An entirely different literary experience that has kept me chuckling in the car and walking with a headset for many delightful hours..."
—Holt Uncensored

Available wherever books and audiobooks are sold.
Fair Oaks Audio • 0-9658811-7-2 Cassette • 0-9658811-6-4 CD